A Letter to Father Christmas

Story by Rose Impey

Pictures by Sue Porter

ORCHARD BOOKS

London

For
Charlotte
x x x x

Text © Rose Impey 1988
Illustrations © Sue Porter 1988
Designed by Sue Porter for Orchard Books
First published in Great Britain in 1988 by
ORCHARD BOOKS
10 Golden Square, London W1R 3AF
Orchard Books Australia
14 Mars Road, Lane Cove NSW 2066
Orchard Books Canada
20 Torbay Road, Markham, Ontario 23P 1G6
1 85213 126 8

Printed in Belgium

 The place where Charlotte lived was too small even to be called a village.

There were no other children to play with, except Ben, of course, but he was still a baby. So Charlotte was quite used to spending time on her own. Often she liked to draw, or dress up, or watch television. Or she might go out into the garden and talk to her friends the donkey and the stray cat who sometimes prowled the flowerbeds looking for birds.

But most of all Charlotte liked to write.

Sometimes Charlotte wrote:

Bread
carrots
fish
Nuts
Milk
Hot water bottle

Or she wrote:

Charlotte Hall
7 Warren Lane
East Kilby
EA3 6PO

Once she even wrote:

Mrs. Hall,
    You need a new
washer on your
stopcock – will bring
one tomorrow.
            Mr. Pipes

Charlotte didn't know that was what she had written because she couldn't read yet. But she could write beautifully. She copied anything she could find and she decorated her writing with tiny drawings.

Today Charlotte was writing something very special– her letter to Father Christmas. She copied carefully from Mum's writing.

Dear Father Christmas,
I am writing to tell you what I would
like in my stocking. When you come
to my house on Christmas Eve you
mustn't look for me in my bedroom
because Grandma and Grandad
will be there. I will be in Ben's room
(next to the bathroom). Ben is too
small to write his own letter so I have
put some things for him on my list.
Also would you bring me a surprise?
I like surprises best of all.
Lots of love, Miss Charlotte Ruth Hall. X

And then, since it was such a long letter, she copied out her Christmas list on a separate piece of paper.

Just as she finished Mum said, "It'll be time for tea soon, Charlie. Tidy up, please."

But unfortunately Charlotte didn't tidy up. Although she did very neat writing, she wasn't always tidy in other ways. Sometimes there was so much clutter on her table that she couldn't even find room to write. Today a pile of paper spilled over onto the floor and that was how Charlotte came to make her terrible mistake.

When Dad woke up Charlotte climbed onto his knee and held out the letter.

"Thank you," said Dad. "Is that for me?"

"No, silly," she said. "It's my letter to Father Christmas."

"Well, it doesn't say so," said Dad. And he showed her how to address it.

to Father Christmas
1, Northpole Lane,
Frostbite,
The Far North,
FC1 0JC.

"Now can we send it?" Charlotte asked.

"OK," said Dad. "You sit back while I post it up the chimney."

Then Dad poked up the fire until there was a strong draught. When he held the letter for a moment above the flames Charlotte caught her breath. She felt sure it would burn. But it didn't.

When Dad let go it flew straight up the chimney and out into the dark night sky. Charlotte raced to the window to watch it, but the letter had already disappeared. It was far away on its journey to Father Christmas.

When Father Christmas opened Charlotte's letter his first thought was, 'Now that's what I call beautiful writing.' But when he came to the list he stopped and read it more carefully.

"This is very odd," he said, pulling at his beard and curling it round his finger.

Father Christmas was used to being asked for all sorts of strange things but he had never been sent a list of presents quite like this.

'Why, it looks more like somebody's shopping list,' he thought. And of course that's exactly what it was.

From then on Mum was even more busy than usual. Grandma and Grandad arrived and the preparations for Christmas really began.

For Charlotte the next few days were a strange mixture. She felt like bursting out laughing one minute and bursting out crying the next.

Everyone else was very busy but Charlotte couldn't settle to anything.

One morning she wandered around the house and leaned
against a window, sucking her thumb. It was then that
she saw the first teasing flakes of snow, there one minute,
disappeared the next. She stared hard, willing it to
fall faster.

"Come on," she whispered. "Snow!"

 So on Christmas Eve morning Charlotte was tired and quieter than usual.

"I hope you're not going to be poorly for Christmas," said Mum.

But Charlotte wasn't poorly, she was still worrying about the animals. Several times that day she tried to get someone to stop what they were doing, to give her some food for them. But everyone said the same thing.

"Ask me later, sweetheart. You can see I'm busy just now."

And they went on being busy all day, right up until the evening.

When the work was finally done, everyone came and sat quietly together round the fire while Grandma read Charlotte the Christmas story. And at last it was time for bed. Charlotte left a mince-pie and a glass of sherry for Father Christmas and hung up her stocking. Then she knew, that after all the waiting, Christmas was really here.

She lay in bed, too excited to sleep, wondering what she would find in her stocking when she woke in the morning. Suddenly she remembered the birds and animals; she still hadn't fed them. Charlotte didn't know what to do. She felt so sad.

A large tear plopped onto her pillow. She wondered if Father Christmas ever brought anything for the animals. If she was Father Christmas she would. Charlotte sucked her thumb. Now she didn't feel excited; she felt rather unhappy.

But by midnight, when Father Christmas tiptoed into her room, Charlotte was fast asleep and dreaming. He leaned over to have a look at her. He was particularly interested to see this little girl who had sent him such an unusual Christmas list.

"I hope you won't be disappointed," he whispered.

On Christmas morning it was just light when
Charlotte woke. She crept out of bed to find her
stocking. It was full and very heavy. But, even before
she opened it, she drew back the curtains. She looked
out onto the garden, hoping to see her animal friends. It
had stopped snowing at last. Everything was icy cold
and sparkling. Only the birds were awake, cutting
clean arrow-shaped tracks across the lawn.

Charlotte crept back into her warm bed and pulled her stocking onto her knee. She took out the first parcel. It was an unusual shape. She felt it. Her fingers pressed into the sides, which were soft and spongy. She took out the next present and shook it. There was a funny slopping noise. And the next one had a strange smell.

Charlotte began to open them. She couldn't believe her eyes. They were not the toys and books she had expected. They were far more unusual presents than that. She unwrapped them one by one...

bread . . .

carrots . . .

fish . . .

nuts . . .

milk . . .

and a hot water bottle.

It was just as if Father Christmas had been able to read her mind. He'd brought her exactly what she needed.

When Mum and Dad woke much later
and went to look in on Charlotte, she wasn't
there. She was already out and about
delivering a few presents of her own.

And Father Christmas hadn't forgotten Charlotte's surprise. At the bottom of her stocking was the perfect present for a little girl who liked to look after animals.